Monday I Was a
Monkey
a "tail" of reverence

To Aiden,
Are you as fast
as a cheetah?
Jennie McC

Jennifer Eichelberger

To Conner, the original monkey
-Jennie McClain

To Anna, for taking care of my monkey
while I illustrated the pictures I hope will
touch many more monkeys who open
these pages
-Jennifer Eichelberger

All Illustrations © Jennifer Eichelberger.

Cover design copyright © 2011 by Covenant Communications, Inc.

Published by Covenant Communications, Inc.
American Fork, Utah

Printed in Korea
First Printing: August 2011

17 16 15 14 13 12 11   10 9 8 7 6 5 4 3 2 1

ISBN-13: 978-1-60861-243-7

Monday I Was a Monkey
a "tail" of reverence

written by
Jennie McClain

illustrated by
Jennifer Eichelberger

Monday I was a monkey.
I ate bananas for breakfast.

Tuesday I was a cheetah.
I ran so fast no one could catch me.

Then I lay down in the bushes to hide, and no one could find me.

Wednesday I was a kangaroo. I carried all my special treasures in a pocket.

I jumped and jumped until I touched the sky.

Thursday I was a bird.
I dug in the dirt, looking for worms.

Friday I was a lion.
I roared so loud I made Mom jump.

I stretched out long
and rolled in the grass.

Saturday I was an elephant. I stomped my feet and made the ground shake.

Sunday I'm just me. I put on my best shirt and pants. I let Mom comb my hair and tie my shoes and tie.

On Sunday I go to church, and
I leave all my animals at home.

I walk quietly down the hall. I keep my arms folded and my footsteps soft.

I sit quietly and listen.
I'm reverent when I'm at church.